Felix the Fluffy Kitten

"Oh, they're all lovely!" Jodie said, as five tiny kittens played about her feet. There were three fluffy grey kittens, like their mum, and two sweet black and white ones with pink noses.

Jodie sighed deeply. "I'm *never* going to be able to choose!"

Lucy the Lonely Kitten

"You're coming home with us, Lucy," said Charlie happily, scratching the top of the kitten's head.

"But I can't leave Rosie behind!" Lucy mewed.

"I want to come too!" Rosie yowled.

But no one was taking any notice.

Also from Macmillan Children's Books

Jenny Dale's KITTEN TALES™

A Kitten Tales Two-Books-in-One Special!

Felix the Fluffy Kitten
Lucy the Lonely Kitten

by Jenny Dale

Illustrated by Susan Hellard

A Working Partners Book

MACMILLAN CHILDREN'S BOOKS

Felix the Fluffy Kitten first published 1999 and *Lucy the Lonely Kitten* first published 2000 by Macmillan Children's Books

This edition first published 2005 by Macmillan Children's Books
a division of Macmillan Publishers Limited
20 New Wharf Road, London N1 9RR
Basingstoke and Oxford
www.panmacmillan.com

Associated companies throughout the world

ISBN 1 405 05576 6

1 3 5 7 9 8 6 4 2

A CIP catalogue record for this book is available from
the British Library.

Typeset by SX Composing DTP, Rayleigh, Essex
Printed and bound in Great Britain by Mackays of Chatham plc, Kent

Felix the Fluffy Kitten

Special thanks to Mary Hooper

To Daisy – another fluffy kitten

Chapter One

Jodie Taylor woke with a start and remembered what day it was. She jumped out of bed and ran straight downstairs in her pyjamas.

"Happy birthday, sleepy head!" her mum said as Jodie bounced into the kitchen. "I was just about to come and wake you up. Fancy sleeping in late today!"

"I was awake at five o'clock, wondering what presents I'd get," Jodie said, rubbing her eyes. "But then I snoozed off again."

Jodie's dad came into the kitchen with his coat on. "Happy birthday, love!" He looked at his watch. "I'll just about have time to watch you open your presents."

Jodie looked excitedly at the pile of cards and presents beside her cereal bowl. She sat down and began opening them.

There was a soft pink sweater from her nana, a computer game from Uncle Jack and a rucksack in the shape of a lamb from Auntie

Joyce. But nothing from her mum and dad.

Jodie looked at them, surprised. Then her dad winked at her mum. What was going on?

"Now open the cards!" he said.

Jodie tore open her cards. There were eight of them – the same number as her new age.

At the bottom of the pile was an ordinary-looking brown envelope with Jodie's name on it. "This doesn't look like a card," she said.

Mr Taylor peered at it. "It doesn't look like anything much."

"Looks like a bill," said Mrs Taylor, trying not to smile.

Jodie opened the envelope and

pulled out a small white square of paper. On it was written:

IOU one kitten.

Jodie looked at her mum and dad in astonishment. "What does this mean?"

"It means," said Mrs Taylor,

smiling, "that your dad and I owe you one birthday kitten – and we're going to collect it later."

Jodie gave a squeal of delight. "Really?" This was what she'd dreamed of for ages. But her mum and dad had always said no. Until now!

Mr Taylor did up his coat. "Mum's taking you to see a lady called Mrs Dent after school," he said. "She has a litter of kittens ready to go to new homes." He dropped a kiss on Jodie's head. "Got to rush. Have a lovely day!" And he left to go to work.

"A kitten," Jodie breathed. "A real live kitten." She gave her mum a hug.

Mrs Taylor smiled, then she

said, "Dad and I think you're old enough now to look after a pet of your own, Jodie."

"Oh, I am, I am!" Jodie said.

"So it's up to you to look after the kitten," Mrs Taylor went on. "You know how busy Dad and I are at the moment. We don't have time to feed and groom a pet or . . ." she pulled a face ". . . clear up any messes."

"Oh, there won't be any messes," Jodie said. She knew lots about pets and loved reading stories about cats. "Kittens are really clean. They're house-trained by their mothers from the moment they're born."

"I'm glad to hear it," said Mrs Taylor as she swished around the sink and gave it a little extra polish. "Because you know I can't bear any mess."

Jodie, used to her mum's neat and tidy ways, hardly heard her. She was getting a kitten! She was getting a kitten of her very own. She could hardly wait!

Chapter Two

"Oh, they're all lovely!" Jodie said, as five tiny kittens played about her feet. There were three fluffy grey kittens, like their mum, and two sweet black and white ones with pink noses.

Jodie sighed deeply. "I'm *never* going to be able to choose!" She got down on the floor and picked up each kitten in turn. "Oh, I don't know!" she wailed.

Jodie's mum smiled. "Can you help, Mrs Dent?"

"They're all good, clean little kittens," Mrs Dent said. "But the short-haired black and whites would be easier to care for. The grey kittens, being long-haired, will need lots more grooming."

"Oh, I won't mind doing that," Jodie said. "I shall love combing *my* kitten." She held up one of the grey fluffies. "This one has the bluest eyes. And he's *really* fluffy!"

The kitten looked at Jodie and miaowed. *Choose me!*

Jodie laughed and put him down so she could look at the

other kittens again. But she kept coming back to the fluffiest one.

The kitten went up to Jodie and rubbed his face against her ankle. "You look nice," he purred. "I'd miss my mum and my brothers and sisters – but I wouldn't mind coming home with you."

"I really think you'll have to

make up your mind, love," Jodie's mum said. "I'm sure Mrs Dent has other things to do."

Jodie watched as the kittens tumbled about, each trying to look the sweetest.

"Come on, Jodie," said Mrs Taylor.

The fluffiest kitten climbed onto Jodie's trainer, mewing up at her. And . . . well, if a kitten could smile, he was doing it.

Jodie's heart melted. "OK, I want . . ." She took a deep breath then scooped up the fluffiest kitten. "This one! I love him to bits already."

Delighted, the kitten pushed his head into Jodie's neck. "Good choice," he purred.

"At last!" said Mrs Taylor.

"What are you going to call him, dear?" Mrs Dent asked, smiling.

Jodie thought hard. "I'm going to call him Felix," she said. She gave Felix a cuddle. "You're my fluffy Felix."

Tired from all his kitten capers, Felix closed his eyes, burrowed his nose into the crook of Jodie's arm and went to sleep.

Jodie's mum paid Mrs Dent, and Felix was put in the pet carrying box they'd bought from the local pet shop on the way.

Jodie looked down at her sleeping kitten and smiled. "Look," she said. "He's so fluffy that you can hardly tell which way round he is!"

"He does have a wonderful thick coat," Mrs Dent agreed. "The thickest I've ever seen. You'll need a special comb for grooming him. And he'll need combing every day." She wrote down the details for Jodie.

Jodie thanked her and gave Felix a gentle stroke before

closing the carrying box.

Still sleeping, Felix purred. What a lovely life he was going to have with his new family . . .

On the way home, Jodie and her mum popped into Pearce's Perfect Pets in the high street.

"Oh, you've brought your new kitten in to see me," said Mr Pearce, the owner.

Felix allowed himself to be lifted out of his basket, put on the counter and shown off to Mr Pearce.

"Well!" said Mr Pearce. "What a fine kitten – and such a wonderful coat."

Felix preened himself, purring loudly. He could get used to all this praise!

Jodie nodded, pleased. "He's lovely, isn't he?"

"You don't want to sell him, do you?" Mr Pearce joked.

"No way!" Jodie said. "We've come in to buy a special comb for grooming long-haired cats." She gave Mr Pearce the piece of paper Mrs Dent had given her, with the

type of comb written on it.

"I don't think I've got one in stock," said Mr Pearce. "But I'll order one for you. Jot down your phone number and I'll ring you when it's in."

"I hope it won't take long," Jodie's mum said, writing down their number. "I want that grey fluff combed out before it gets shed all over the house!"

Mr Pearce tickled Felix behind his ears. "With a thick coat like that, I reckon you'd soon comb enough fluff off him to knit yourself a woolly jumper!" he joked.

Jodie laughed. "I just want to keep him looking good."

"I tell you what," Mr Pearce

said. "He's such a handsome kitten that I'd like to take his photograph to put in my window. I'm sure it would attract a lot of attention. I'll give you the comb and a smart new collar in return. How's that?"

"Great!" said Jodie. "Can we, Mum?"

Mrs Taylor nodded. "I can't see why not," she said.

Felix began to wash around his face so that he'd look his best for the photograph.

"Why don't you choose a collar while I go and get my camera?" said Mr Pearce.

Jodie held a red and a green collar next to Felix, then chose the red one. She was carefully putting it on him when Mr Pearce came back with his camera.

Felix just loved attention. Everyone in the shop was watching him now. "How about this?" he purred, looking over his shoulder, his tail up straight. "Or this?" he miaowed, rolling on his back and looking up at the camera, his blue eyes wide. "Have you ever seen anything so sweet?"

"I think he knows he's being snapped," Mr Pearce said, grinning. "He's posing like a model. He thinks he's one of those supermodels."

Supermodel? Superkitten, more like, Felix thought.

Chapter Three

"You'll have to try to keep Felix off this sofa, Jodie," Mrs Taylor said a couple of days later.

Jodie had just come in from school and was sitting watching TV, with Felix on her lap.

Mrs Taylor dabbed at the sofa with a damp cloth, then frowned at the grey fluff she'd gathered up. "Dad sat down wearing his new suit and got it covered in grey hairs this morning," she went on.

"Sorry," Jodie said. "I'll try and brush some of the loose fluff out of Felix's coat later." She was going to make do with an old blue hairbrush until the special comb arrived at the pet shop.

Tutting a little under her breath, Mrs Taylor went over to the vacuum cleaner in the corner. "And this old vacuum cleaner of ours is hopeless!" she added.

"Shall I have a go with it?" Jodie offered, feeling guilty at the extra work Felix's fluff was making for her mum.

Mrs Taylor shook her head. "It's much too heavy for you to lug around, love. It's too heavy for me, come to that!" She plugged in the big old machine and switched it on.

Felix, who'd been snoozing, sat bolt upright. *What* was that horrible roaring noise? He jumped down and made a dash for the stairs. Pale grey fluff hung in the air as he ran . . .

It was Saturday and Jodie was taking her time in the bathroom. She didn't have to rush to school this morning and could play with her new kitten all day.

Felix had decided to keep Jodie company while she showered,

and was perched on the edge of the bath. He bobbed from side to side, dabbing his paw in the drops of water. "Why can't I catch these little round silvery things?" he miaowed sharply. It was very annoying!

Jodie turned off the shower and put a dollop of soapy foam on the edge of the bath for Felix to play with.

Felix looked at the white froth. He reached out a paw – but the bit he touched seemed to disappear. Very odd.

He leaned over to sniff the strange stuff – and jumped back in surprise, sneezing as tiny soapy bubbles flew up his nose. Felix lost his balance and slid into

the bath, a wisp of foam still on his nose.

"Oh, Felix!" Jodie cried. "You silly puss!"

Jodie couldn't stop laughing as she lifted Felix out of the bath.

Then she noticed the hairs that had flown off Felix as he'd skidded into the bath. She grabbed a cloth and quickly wiped them up before her mum noticed. Jodie could hear the vacuum cleaner on again, downstairs.

Felix had been with the Taylors for just over a week now, and he had settled in really well. But there was one big problem: his fluff!

Felix's lovely thick coat shed oodles of fluffy hair wherever Felix went. And Mrs Taylor was *not* pleased about it.

Jodie got dressed and took Felix into her bedroom. "Time to brush out some of that fluff," she said to him, setting him down on her bed.

She went to find the old blue hairbrush. But when she came

back, Felix had vanished. Then
she noticed a fluffy tail, fat as a
squirrel's, sticking out of the
duvet. "I can see you!" she called.

Jodie flung back the duvet to
find Felix crouched down ready
to pounce. He leapt into the air,
scrabbled up her back and landed
on her shoulder. "You're back!

Let's play!" he miaowed loudly.

As Jodie collapsed onto the bed, giggling, her mum appeared in the doorway.

"Just look at all that fluff on your bedclothes, Jodie," Mrs Taylor said frowning. "You'd better change them. And don't you think it's about time you started grooming that kitten? If you combed out all that loose fluff it wouldn't come out all over the house!"

"I'm going to, Mum – right now," Jodie said, and held up the brush to show her.

With a sigh, Mrs Taylor went back to her cleaning. Pulling Felix onto her lap, Jodie gently began to stroke the brush along his back.

But as far as Felix was concerned, the bristly blue creature was trying to attack him! He sprang round. "How dare you!" he hissed, ready to fight the brush.

Jodie sighed. "Come on, Felix, you have to let me groom you – otherwise we'll *both* be in trouble!"

Just then, the vacuum cleaner stopped again, and Mrs Taylor called from the bathroom. "Jodie, leave that kitten alone for a moment and come in here, will you?"

Jodie put the brush down on the bed and went out to her mum. Felix pounced on the blue creature, biting and kicking it.

"Caught you!" he growled happily.

"Have you had Felix in here with you?" Jodie's mum asked sternly when Jodie went into the bathroom.

Jodie nodded. "He likes to sit and watch me clean my teeth."

"I thought so," Mrs Taylor said, "because there are hairs in the sink *and* on the flannels." Mrs Taylor shook her head. "Wherever I look there's a smudge of grey fluff!"

"But what can I do, Mum?" Jodie said. "Felix can't help moulting."

"I never seem to stop cleaning these days," Mrs Taylor

grumbled. "Not since Felix arrived." And then she stared at a toothbrush in horror. "That's the limit!" she cried. "There's cat hair on my toothbrush!"

"Perhaps the special comb we've ordered from the pet shop will work," Jodie said.

Her mum nodded. "I hope so – I feel quite worn out with all the extra work."

Feeling guilty, Jodie escaped back to her bedroom and watched as Felix burrowed under her duvet again, leaving a cloud of grey fluff behind him. She just hoped that Felix would allow her to use the new comb on him. If he didn't, she could see things getting *very* difficult . . .

Chapter Four

A couple of days later, Jodie and her mum made their way to Pearce's Perfect Pets after school. Mr Pearce had called to say the special comb was in.

As they approached the pet shop Jodie noticed that Felix's photograph was now in the window. "Oh, look, Mum!" she pointed. "There's Felix! Doesn't he look gorgeous?"

They both stopped and stared at the big photograph of Felix in the middle of the window display. He was wearing his new collar, with his head on one side, looking his cutest. A slogan above the picture read:

POSH PETS COME TO PEARCE'S

Mrs Taylor nodded. "Yes, he looks lovely." Then she gave a little sigh. "But sometimes I can't help wishing that you'd chosen one of the short-haired kittens."

"Don't say that, Mum!" Jodie

protested. "I love Felix. He's the most beautiful kitten in the world!"

"He's certainly the fluffiest!" said Mrs Taylor. And then she smiled. "He *is* gorgeous, and I'm awfully fond of him. But he makes such a lot of mess!"

As they went into the shop, Jodie looked once more at the

beautiful photograph of Felix. Who would have thought that choosing the fluffiest kitten would cause such a lot of problems?

"I *wish* you'd let me comb you, Felix!" Jodie said. "It might help with all the fluff, you know."

"Purreow!" Felix said. "I've decided I don't like those things called brushes and combs – they mess up my lovely fur."

Jodie had tried the special comb for long-haired cats for the first time yesterday. But it hadn't been a great success. Felix treated it just like the blue hairbrush.

As he rolled on the carpet, showing his soft fluffy tummy,

Jodie put her hand out for the comb. Half-hiding it in her hand, she very gently combed down his tummy with it and collected some soft fluff in its plastic teeth.

Felix sprang to life. *That* thing again! "Miaow!" He jumped on it, caught it and gave it a good old bite.

"Oh, *Felix*!" Jodie cried, pulling the comb away from him. It already had tiny teeth marks in the handle, where Felix had attacked it yesterday. His kitten teeth were sharp as needles.

"Oh, don't you want to play, then?" Felix miaowed.

Jodie sighed as she heard the monster cleaner roaring away downstairs again. "Maybe you'll let me groom you when you get older," she said.

Felix stared up at her with his bright blue eyes. No, he didn't think so . . .

Just then, the doorbell rang downstairs and the vacuum cleaner was hastily switched off. As Mrs Taylor opened the door,

Jodie could hear a very familiar voice. Then her mum called upstairs.

"Jodie! Mrs Oberon's here. Come and say hello!"

Jodie gathered Felix up. "Mrs Oberon is organising the school fête this year," she told him. "She's my teacher. She's a bit posh and strict – but quite nice really."

"Of course I'd be delighted to help at the school fête," Mrs Taylor was saying, as Jodie carried Felix into the sitting room. "Just let me know what you'd like me to do."

The smartly-dressed visitor was sitting on the sofa. "Oh thank you!" she said. Then she smiled at Jodie. "Hello, Jodie – lovely kitten!" she added, seeing Felix. "Maybe we should have a cat competition at the fête. He'd be bound to win!"

Felix purred with pleasure. He liked Mrs Oberon.

Jodie and her mum showed Mrs Oberon to the door, then waited until their guest had reached the front gate.

Suddenly, Mrs Taylor gasped. "Oh no!"

"What?" Jodie asked, puzzled.

"Mrs Oberon's skirt!" Mrs Taylor whispered.

"What about it?" Jodie asked, even more puzzled. She hadn't noticed anything strange about it.

"Didn't you see?" said her

mum, closing the door. "All down the back of it – grey fluff!"

Jodie went into the sitting room to look at the sofa. There was fluff all over the cushions again. She hurriedly tried to brush it off.

"I thought I told you not to let that kitten on the sofa!" Mrs Taylor thundered.

Felix, who was still sitting on the sofa, took one look at Mrs Taylor's angry face and disappeared underneath it.

"This is so embarrassing!" Jodie's mum went on. "What on earth will Mrs Oberon think when she gets home and sees her skirt covered in fluff?" Jodie didn't really think there was anything wrong with having cat

fluff on your skirt. Or on the carpet or the sofa, or in the bath. But her mum sighed heavily. "This is the last straw! I'm beginning to think that kitten of yours ought to live in the garage, you know."

"Mum!" Jodie protested. "We can't do that – he'd hate it!"

Felix, lying flat underneath the sofa, gave a frightened squeak. This was going too far! A kitten – a *super*kitten like him – couldn't possibly live in a *garage*.

"Well, I just can't think of another solution," Mrs Taylor said. "He refuses to be groomed, he won't stay off the furniture . . . and all I do is clean the place morning, noon and night!"

"But, Mum—" Jodie was just about to start pleading with her mum when the phone rang.

"Bill Pearce here, lass," a voice said when Jodie answered it. "From Pearce's Perfect Pets. How's your fluffy kitten?"

"Er . . . he's OK," Jodie said, looking at her mum, who was

still frowning and was about to start vacuuming again.

"And did the new comb do the trick?" Mr Pearce asked.

"Not exactly," Jodie said uncomfortably.

"Well, it's about that – about the fluff – that I'm ringing you," Mr Pearce went on. "Can I have a word with your mum?"

Jodie handed the phone to Mrs Taylor, who spoke with Mr Pearce for a while.

Then she put the phone down, looking puzzled. "Mr Pearce says that he has some people in his shop who want to meet Felix," she said.

Hearing his name, Felix gave a mew of alarm and crawled to the

very back of the sofa. What was happening *now*?

"What's it about, Mum?" Jodie asked, surprised.

"He wouldn't say," Mrs Taylor replied. "But they're coming round straight away." She switched on the vacuum cleaner. "It all sounds most mysterious."

Chapter Five

"Hello," Jodie said shyly, as Mr Pearce brought a small, smiling man and a tall woman with frizzy red hair into the house.

"This is Mr Tomkins and his assistant, Miss Spark," said Mr Pearce.

"Pleased to meet you," said

Jodie's mum, shaking hands with them. "Although I can't think why you wanted to meet Felix."

Felix was watching from underneath the sofa. What did these people want with him?

"If I may explain," Mr Tomkins said, stepping forward. "My assistant, Miss Spark here, visited Mr Pearce's shop a few days ago and admired the photograph of Felix in the window . . ."

Felix, with a soft miaow, came out from under the sofa. "Here I am!"

The two visitors gave an "*Aaah!*" of admiration.

"Oh, how sweet!" Miss Spark cried. Her red curls bobbed round her pointy face. "Mr Pearce told me that Felix was the fluffiest kitten he'd ever seen!" she said.

"And I'm pleased to see he's very fluffy indeed," Mr Tomkins added.

Jodie picked up Felix and stroked him proudly. A small shower of grey fluff floated out from his coat. Everyone watched as it slowly sank to the floor. Jodie's heart sank too. Was her mum going to be angry?

"Ahem . . ." said Miss Spark. "Mr Pearce also told me you were having a spot of trouble with Felix's fluff."

"Well, yes," said Mrs Taylor. She glanced at Jodie. "It's true that all I seem to do these days is clean up after Felix. I've got a vacuum

cleaner but it's not really up to the job."

"And that is why we're here!" boomed Mr Tomkins happily.

"Shall I go and get it, sir?" Miss Spark asked, a hint of excitement in her voice.

Mr Tomkins nodded. "If you don't mind, Miss Spark."

Miss Spark went to the white van parked outside. She came back in carrying a strange, shiny machine. Written on the side, in bright blue letters, was *Wizard*.

"It looks like a robot!" Jodie said, staring at the large silver box with arms attached.

Felix jumped down from Jodie's arms and approached the machine. What a strange-looking creature! He saw himself in the shiny surface. "Miiaoww!" What a fine-looking kitten!

"This," said Mr Tomkins proudly, "is my latest invention. It's not *just* a vacuum cleaner..."

Felix backed away from the silver creature. "Is *that* a vacuum cleaner?" he miaowed.

". . . It's *the* vacuum cleaner!" Mr Tomkins continued. "Better than any other!" He beamed at Jodie and her mum. "I've called it the Wizard because it can clean any house like magic!"

"Really?" Mrs Taylor looked at it wistfully. "Well, it looks very good, but—"

Mr Tomkins held up his hand. "Please allow us to demonstrate . . ." He turned to his assistant. "Miss Spark, would you plug in the Wizard, please?"

"Certainly, Mr Tomkins," his assistant replied. By now, Miss Spark's red curls seemed to fizz with excitement.

Felix wondered if he should make a dash for it. He'd heard

the dreaded words "vacuum cleaner", and that usually meant trouble.

But while he was deciding, Miss Spark switched the machine on. The silver creature began to hum.

Felix sat with his head on one side and stared, puzzled. Why wasn't it making a nasty loud roaring sound like Mrs Taylor's vacuum cleaner?

Miss Spark began to put the machine through its paces, moving one of its long rubbery arms over the sofa.

"Look at that!" Mrs Taylor cried, delighted. The sofa cushions looked brand new!

Then Miss Spark pushed the machine across the carpet. "With

one gentle push, the Wizard slides easily along the floor, picking up every single hair as it passes," she said.

"It picks up fluff you didn't know you had!" Mr Tomkins joked.

Felix watched the humming silver creature gliding smoothly along the carpet. It didn't seem fierce, like the other vacuum cleaner. And he did like being able to see himself in the creature's shiny body. Perhaps he should make friends with it.

Felix ran towards the machine, jumped on it and pawed at his reflection.

"Felix looks as if he's driving it!" Jodie laughed.

Everyone smiled, watching Felix as he sat on the Wizard like a figurehead. His purring was almost as loud as the Wizard's hum.

As Miss Spark steered the Wizard past Jodie, Felix looked up. "Hey, Jodie!" he miaowed. "This is fun!"

53

Mrs Taylor shook her head in awe, looking at the spotless sofa and carpet. "I've never seen the place looking so clean," she said. "At least, not since Felix has been here."

Jodie had to agree.

"And finally," said Miss Spark as she switched the vacuum cleaner off, "the Wizard also sucks fluff and dust from the air – before it has a chance to settle."

"That's fantastic!" Jodie said.

As the machine stopped moving, Felix stepped off and sat next to his new friend, his head on one side.

Mr Pearce began clapping. "It looks as though Felix thinks he's done the cleaning himself," he said.

"He's an absolute darling!" Miss Spark cried.

Felix was really enjoying himself. Everyone seemed to think he was great! And now that his silver friend had cleaned up all his fluff, perhaps Mrs Taylor would forget about banishing him to the garage.

But Jodie's mum was looking worried again. "It's a marvellous machine," she said. "I'd love one – but I'm afraid we simply can't afford a new vacuum cleaner. Especially such an expensive-looking one . . ."

"Oh, I don't want you to *buy* one!" Mr Tomkins said.

Chapter Six

"What?" Mrs Taylor said in surprise.

"Let me explain," said Mr Tomkins. "We want Felix to star in our advertisements," he said.

Jodie gasped.

"He's a natural," Mr Tomkins went on. "With Felix showing off the Wizard, we'll sell thousands!"

"Oh, wow!" Jodie cried. She picked up Felix and hugged him. "You're going to be famous!" she whispered.

Felix rubbed his head against Jodie's neck. "Great!" he purred. "I've always wanted to be a superkitten."

"I can see the posters now," Mr Tomkins said, rubbing his hands together happily. "They'll say: *Buy a Wizard – the ultimate fluffbuster!*"

"Or how about: *So quiet it won't even frighten a kitten!*" Miss Spark added.

"Very good, Miss Spark!" Mr Tomkins boomed.

"And: *So light even a kitten can*

push it!" Mr Pearce offered. "If you don't mind me joining in," he added, going a bit red.

"Thank you, Mr Pearce! Another excellent suggestion!" cried Mr Tomkins. Then he turned to Jodie's mum. "We'll pay a fee, of course. And the 'Wizard Kitten' must have a Wizard for his own home. We'll leave this one for you, shall we?"

Jodie and her mum stood there, too astounded to speak. Felix gave a short miaow. "Say yes!" He wanted to be a superkitten. He wanted to be famous – and he wanted it now!

One evening, a few weeks later, Jodie and her mum and dad were all sitting in front of the television. Felix was sitting on Jodie's lap. He was quite a bit bigger, but still very fluffy.

"Mr Tomkins said it would be on at five-thirty," Jodie said. She looked at her watch. "It's nearly that now."

"I only make it twenty-five

past," Mr Taylor said.

Felix looked up at Jodie, his bright blue eyes puzzled. Why was everyone so excited? Even Jodie's dad had come home from work early.

"Have we got the video set?" Mrs Taylor asked.

Just then there was a noise outside in the hall and a cheerful woman put her head around the door. It was Mrs Bell.

Felix turned round and miaowed. "Hello, Mrs Bell." He liked Mrs Bell. Ever since Mr Tomkins had paid a lot of money for Felix's kitten modelling, Mrs Bell had been coming here to do all the cleaning.

"I've finished cleaning

upstairs," Mrs Bell said. "Do you want me to do in here now?"

"Oh, Mrs Bell," said Jodie's mum, smiling. "Come and watch the advertisement first! It should be on any min—"

She was interrupted by a scream from Jodie. "Here he is! Oh, look, Felix, there you are!"

Jodie held Felix up in front of the television and he saw himself sitting proudly on a Wizard as it was put through its paces.

"Solve even the fluffiest problem with the aid of your Wizard!" said a voice on the TV. *"Cleans your home like magic!"*

"Don't you look gorgeous!" Jodie cried.

"Purreow!" said Felix. He

jumped down and sat as close to the TV as he could, staring up at himself. "Yes, I do look pretty good . . ."

As the advertisement ended, everyone sighed with pride. Then Felix gave a tiny sneeze and shook himself, sending a shower of fluffy grey fur into the air.

Jodie laughed. "You can do that as much as you like, Felix," she said. "Because now you're getting paid for it!"

Lucy the Lonely Kitten

Special thanks to Narinder Dhami

Chapter One

"Look out, Rosie!" Lucy miaowed. "Here I come!" The little black kitten leaped off the ledge at the side of the pen, almost landing right on top of her sister.

"You did that on purpose!" Rosie miaowed back. She was

black too, but had a white splodge under her chin and two white paws. "I'm going to get you for that!" She playfully bashed Lucy's ear with her paw, then pounced on her sister's swishing tail.

Lucy and Rosie rolled around, locked together in one furry ball, nipping playfully at each other. They had lived at the animal shelter all their lives, sharing their big pen with three older cats – Ginger, Tammy and Winston. The other cats were snoozing in the sun at the moment, and taking absolutely no notice of the kittens. But Lucy and Rosie were used to that. They tumbled happily around the pen, stopping

only when they heard voices
coming towards them.

"Have a good look round, and if
you see a kitten you like, let me
know."

Lucy and Rosie both pricked up
their ears. That was John, who
ran the animal shelter and looked
after them all. And it sounded

like someone had come to choose a kitten to take home with them! A new owner was what most of the animals in the shelter were waiting for, and Lucy and Rosie both rushed to the front of their pen, purring hopefully.

A little girl and her parents were walking slowly along the line of pens, peering into each one. Some of the cats and kittens took no notice. Many of them were used to being disappointed in their search for a new home.

Lucy and Rosie, in the very last pen, waited impatiently for the visitors to reach them.

"Come and see us," they purred. "We're lovely. And we're looking for a nice new home!"

"There are so many to choose from," said the girl, her eyes wide. "I wish I could take them *all* home with me!"

Her mother laughed. "I know we've got more room in the house now that Sam's left home," she said. "But I don't think we've got enough space for *all* of them!"

"Do you see one you like, Charlie?" asked her father.

Charlie looked carefully up and down the row of pens. She'd been waiting for a kitten for so long now, she could hardly believe she was getting one at last. She'd been feeling very miserable today, until her parents had surprised her by saying that she could get a kitten.

Charlie's older sister Sam had left home that morning, and gone away to college. Charlie and Sam argued a lot of the time (especially when Charlie borrowed Sam's CDs without asking), but Charlie really hadn't wanted her sister to go.

They had all gone to take Sam to her new flat, squeezing into the car that was packed to the roof with Sam's belongings.

"See you, trouble!" Sam had said, giving Charlie a hug.

"See you," said Charlie. She didn't cry very often, but she'd had to bite her lip then.

And when they'd got home, Sam's bedroom had looked *very* empty with all her posters and books and CDs missing.

But at least Charlie was getting a kitten! She had passed the animal shelter at the end of their road every day on her way to school. And always, she wished she could have a pet of her own.

Charlie cheered up even more as she peered into the cages. That ginger kitten was very pretty, and there was a tiny white one which was curled up asleep in the sun. Charlie just didn't have a clue which one to choose as she reached the last pen.

"Hello!" purred Lucy, standing up on her back legs and poking one little paw through the wire mesh. Rosie did the same, staring up at Charlie.

"Oh, these two are cute!" Charlie said. She bent down and pushed a finger through the wire. Lucy sniffed at it, while Rosie purred like an engine.

"Mum, can we go in and see these two kittens?" Charlie asked eagerly.

Lucy and Rosie glanced at each other in delight.

Charlie's father went off to fetch John, who came back carrying a large bunch of keys. It took him a long time to find the right key for Lucy and Rosie's pen.

Lucy and Rosie stood waiting impatiently. Even the older cats had opened their eyes to see what was going on. At last, John opened the door and let Charlie in.

"They're gorgeous!" said Charlie happily, as Lucy and Rosie fell over themselves trying to scramble over her trainers. She stroked them, and the kittens purred, pushing their heads against her hands.

"This one's Lucy and that's Rosie," said John with a smile. "They've been with us ever since they were born."

"Well, Charlie?" asked her mother.

Charlie frowned. It was so difficult to choose. She stroked Rosie, then giggled as Lucy attacked the trailing laces of one her trainers. "I think I'll have this one!" And she picked Lucy up and cuddled her.

"What do you mean, you'll have *this* one?" Lucy miaowed, alarmed. "What about Rosie?"

Rosie was looking anxious now too, pawing at Charlie's leg to get her attention.

"You're coming home with us, Lucy," said Charlie happily, scratching the top of the kitten's head.

"But I can't leave Rosie behind!" Lucy mewed.

"I want to come too!" Rosie yowled.

But no one was taking any notice.

"Right, you've already had a home visit from one of our staff and Lucy's had her injections. That means you can take her away with you now," John said briskly. "We'll go and find a box for her, and sort out the paperwork."

Charlie handed Lucy over to John, and they all went out of the pen.

Miaowing pitifully, Rosie tried to follow them, but John shut the door quickly so she couldn't get out.

"Lucy!" Rosie mewed. "Lucy! Don't go without me!"

But there was nothing Lucy could do. John was holding her gently but firmly, too firmly for her to escape. All she could do was miaow miserably as she was carried away, leaving her sister staring sadly after them.

Chapter Two

"Is Lucy all right, Mum?" asked Charlie anxiously as they drew up outside the Carters' house. "She hasn't stopped making a noise since we left the animal shelter."

"She's probably a bit nervous," Mrs Carter replied with a smile.

"Don't forget, all this is very new to her."

Lucy pawed the side of the cardboard carrier. "Why won't anyone listen to me?" she yowled. It was dark inside the box, and she didn't like it at all. "I want my sister!"

"Let's get her inside," said Mr Carter, turning off the engine.

Lucy stopped yowling as she felt herself on the move again. A moment or two later the flaps on top of the box opened, and Charlie reached inside.

"Come and see your new home, Lucy," she said as she lifted the kitten out.

"What about Rosie?" Lucy mewed sadly. But Charlie didn't

understand her, of course. Instead she put the kitten gently down on the living room carpet.

Even though Lucy was still very upset about leaving Rosie behind, after a moment or two she began to look around cautiously. There were lots of new things here to sniff and scratch and explore;

things which hadn't been in the pen at the animal shelter. And there was so much space! Lucy could hardly believe how big the room was. It was *much* bigger than any of the pens at the shelter.

"Look, Lucy." Charlie began to unpack the carrier bags that her father had just brought in from the car. "We went shopping before we came to the animal shelter, and we've bought you lots of things!"

Lucy watched as Charlie emptied out a whole bagful of toys. There were little balls for chasing. Some were soft and squishy, and some had a little bell in the middle which tinkled when

the ball rolled along. There was a
fluffy mouse with a long tail
made of pink wool, and an
enormous furry spider bouncing
up and down on a piece of elastic.

"What about this, Lucy?" said
Charlie, jiggling the spider up
and down in front of the kitten.

Lucy watched politely, but she

didn't really care much about the toys. She hadn't needed any toys at the shelter, because she had had Rosie to play with . . .

Apart from the toys, there was also a very snug-looking cat basket, lined with velvet.

"This is where you're going to sleep, Lucy," said Charlie.

Lucy stared miserably up at Charlie. Until now, she had always slept with Rosie. The two kittens had curled around each other so tightly, it was difficult to tell which was which. But Rosie wasn't here to share the basket with her. Lucy was all alone.

"I wish Sam could see you, Lucy," Charlie whispered. She picked Lucy up and rubbed her chin against her kitten's soft fur. "Sam's my sister, but she doesn't live with us any more. I miss her already."

"I miss *my* sister too!" Lucy yowled.

"What's the matter, Lucy?" Charlie asked worriedly. "Oh, I know! You're probably hungry." And she took Lucy into the kitchen.

"How's she doing now?" asked Mrs Carter, who was making tea.

"She still doesn't seem very happy," Charlie said with a frown. "I thought she might be hungry." She put Lucy down, and spooned some catfood into a bowl. Lucy sniffed the air. The food smelt delicious, and she *was*

hungry. As soon as the bowl was put in front of her, she began to eat quickly.

"Good girl, Lucy," said Charlie, looking relieved. But a moment or two later Lucy stopped eating, and began miaowing again.

"Oh, Lucy," Charlie said, upset. "What's wrong?"

"I'm thinking about Rosie," Lucy mewed sadly. "She might not get much to eat without me to look after her – that Winston can be a bit of a bully sometimes!"

"Mum, what's the matter with her?" Charlie asked.

"Just give her a chance to settle in," Mrs Carter said, gently stroking the kitten's back. "Are you going to carry on calling her Lucy, or are you going to give her another name?"

"No, I like Lucy," said Charlie.

"So do I!" Lucy purred, and she rubbed her head against Charlie's ankles. She was beginning to like Charlie a lot. Charlie had understood that Lucy didn't want a different name. Now all she had to do was make her new owner understand that everything would be perfect if only Rosie could come and live with them too.

Chapter Three

"Lucy, what *is* the matter with you?" Charlie asked, shaking her head sadly. "I wish I knew."

Lucy gave a tiny miaow, and then turned back to stare out of the living room window again.

"That's what she's done all week," said Mrs Carter. "She sits and stares out of the window. And it takes her ages to climb up there." She looked ruefully at the claw marks on the sofa, where Lucy had scrambled up to reach the window. "It's almost as if she's *looking* for someone."

"I *am*," Lucy miaowed sadly. Every day she sat in the window, hoping that John would turn up at the Carters' house with Rosie. They could play with all Lucy's new toys, eat a big bowlful of delicious food and then curl up together in the big comfy basket for a snooze.

But as the days passed, Lucy had begun to realise that Rosie wasn't coming. That made her feel very lonely and miserable indeed, even though Charlie had been very kind to her and had given her everything any kitten could want. Would she ever see her sister again?

"I wish you could talk, Lucy," Charlie sighed, tickling the kitten under her chin. She'd waited for a kitten for so long, and now it seemed as if Lucy didn't even *want* to be Charlie's cat. "Then I could find out what's bothering you."

"I *can* talk!" Lucy mewed. "You just don't understand me, that's all!" She rubbed her fluffy head against Charlie's hand. Lucy liked playing with her new owner, but Charlie had to go to school, and then Lucy got very bored on her own. She was worried about Rosie too. Her sister was shy, and had always relied on Lucy to look after her. Lucy couldn't bear to think of Rosie all alone in the pen at the shelter.

"Why don't you take Lucy out into the back garden?" Charlie's mum suggested. "She's got a collar and identity tag on now, and she's got to get used to going out sometime."

Lucy pricked up her ears. *Out*? Her heart began to thump with excitement. She hadn't been allowed out of the house during the week she'd been there, but if she was let outside, then she would be able to get away and go back to the animal shelter to see Rosie!

Charlie looked doubtful. "I don't want her to get lost."

"Oh, she won't be able to get out of the garden," said Mrs Carter confidently. "The fences are high, and she's far too small to climb them. She'll be quite safe."

"That's what *you* think," Lucy said to herself, feeling very determined. She just *had* to make sure that Rosie was all right – and it looked like she was going to get a chance to do so!

Eagerly, she jumped down off the windowsill and slid down the leg of the sofa, claws extended. Mrs Carter winced.

"I think we'd better get her a scratching-post!" she said, as Lucy rushed over to the door.

Charlie followed Lucy across the room. "Hey, slow down!" she laughed as Lucy skidded across the polished floor of the hall towards the back door.

Lucy scratched at the bottom

of the door, miaowing loudly.

Charlie's face lit up. "You seem a lot happier, Lucy!" she said, looking relieved. "Now don't be scared of going outside," she went on as she unlocked the door. "I'll look after you—"

Charlie didn't get the chance to say any more. As soon as the door opened just a crack, Lucy squeezed through it and rushed outside. Then she stopped on the patio and looked around eagerly, sniffing the air. But what she saw made her heart sink.

The Carters' back garden was surrounded on all sides by very high fences. There didn't seem to be any way out at all, not even a small hole that a kitten could squeeze through. Lucy looked around desperately. If she could only find a way out, she just knew that she'd be able to find her way back to the animal shelter. After all, it was only just up the road.

"Wait for me, Lucy!" Charlie laughed as the kitten suddenly raced off down the lawn.

Lucy didn't stop. She had finally spotted a way of getting out of the garden. It wasn't easy, and it would take all her strength and determination, but she was going to do it!

There were trees all round the edges of the lawn. Most of them were very tall, much too tall for Lucy to climb. She couldn't even have made it onto the very lowest branches. But there was a plant growing in the flower border, and it had grown so much that it had trailed right over the fence and down into the street that ran alongside the garden. Lucy saw that she could get right over the fence, using the thick stems of the climbing plant like a ladder.

Lucy headed straight towards the creeper. She scrambled up the main stem, clinging on with all her might.

"Lucy! What are you doing?" Charlie called, alarmed.

Lucy clung on as hard as she could, beginning to climb higher. It was very scary because although the stems were quite thick, they were also quite floppy. They bent under her weight, even though she was very light. But she kept going.

"Lucy!" Charlie raced over to her, but Lucy was just out of her reach. "Come down!"

Lucy hauled herself up onto the top of the fence. She was panting and shaking, and she had bits of leaves and twigs stuck in her coat, but she'd made it!

She looked over the fence, and was relieved to see that the plant reached almost down to the pavement on the other side.

"Keep still, Lucy!" Charlie called urgently. "I'm going to get Mum!"

Lucy looked down at her owner.

She didn't want to upset Charlie when she'd been so kind to her, but she just had to go and see Rosie! With a little mew of farewell, she disappeared over the fence.

Chapter Four

She'd done it! Lucy dropped
down onto the street on the other
side of the garden. She knew she
had no time to waste. Charlie and
Mrs Carter would soon be hot on
her trail!

Lucy ran off, and then hid
behind a postbox to get her

bearings. She sniffed the air intently, her whiskers twitching as she decided which way to go. Yes, she was sure she could make it to the shelter quite easily. She couldn't wait to see Rosie's face!

Lucy trotted down the street, keeping well away from the traffic. There was so much that was strange and new all around her, but Lucy kept her head down and kept going. She had only one thought in her mind – to make it safely back to Rosie.

"Oh, look, Emma," said a voice above Lucy's head all of a sudden. "Look at that sweet little kitten!"

"Isn't it cute, Natalie!" said another voice.

Lucy glanced up. Two girls were

blocking the pavement in front of her, and she couldn't really get past them. So she waited while they stroked her, and tickled her under the chin.

"I wish I had a cat," said Emma, who was blonde, and wore big-heeled shoes. "He's gorgeous."

He! Lucy thought indignantly, wishing she could be on her way.

"Yeah, he is," agreed Natalie, who was dark-haired and wore baggy tracksuit bottoms. "But isn't he a bit young to be out on his own?"

"You're right," Emma agreed. "We'd better take him back to his owner."

Time for me to go! Lucy thought. She darted forward quickly, right

through Emma's legs, and
streaked off up the road. Both
girls made a grab for her, but
missed.

That was close! Lucy thought, as
she hurried off down the street.

"Hello, Puss," said a milkman
as he came out of one of the
gardens. He put the empty bottles

he was holding on the milk float, and came towards Lucy. "Aren't you a bit young to be out on your own?"

"No, I'm not!" Lucy mewed, and dashed off. She didn't want any more kind people trying to catch her!

A few houses later, she stopped and looked back to check that the milkman wasn't following her – and it was then that she got a real shock.

"Mum! Look what I've found!" said an excited voice, and a pair of hands clamped down on Lucy and picked her up. Lucy struggled frantically and yowled, but she couldn't get away.

"Look, Mum," said the little

boy, who was carrying Lucy. He took her over to his mother, who was weeding their front garden. "I found it outside our gate."

"Oh, what a sweet little kitten!" said his mother, stroking Lucy's head. "But she's very young to be out on her own."

"Maybe she's lost," the boy suggested.

"I'm not lost," Lucy mewed crossly. "I know exactly where I'm going!"

"Well, she's got a collar on with a phone number," said the boy's mother, inspecting Lucy's ID tag. "We'd better ring her owners – they'll be worried."

Lucy struggled helplessly as the boy carried her into the house.

"Let me go!" she wailed. "I'm going to see my sister!"

"The poor little thing must be scared out of its wits," said the boy's mum as they went into the kitchen. "Listen to the noise she's making!"

Lucy gave up. Why couldn't humans understand *anything*?

"We'd better put her somewhere safe, Luke, while I ring the owner," the boy's mum went on. "Go and fetch the cardboard carrier we took Gilbert to the vet in."

"But Gilbert's only a guinea pig," Luke objected. "The box won't be big enough."

"It'll be big enough for a small kitten like that," said his mum.

"No! I don't want to go in there!" Lucy squealed as she was gently lifted into the cardboard carrier. She didn't know what a guinea pig was, but the box smelled very funny indeed.

"It won't be for long," Luke said, patting Lucy on the head before closing the flaps.

Meanwhile, his mum was dialling the Carters' number.

Lucy was in darkness. Well, almost. There was a small hole in one of the corners which was letting a tiny amount of daylight in. Eagerly, Lucy went to investigate. Whatever a guinea pig was, it must have very sharp teeth because Gilbert had begun to chew his way through the

corner of the box. Now all Lucy
had to do was make the hole a
little bit bigger . . .

Lucy began to scratch and
scrape at the hole with her sharp
little claws. The cardboard began
to tear, and the hole grew larger.
And larger. Now Lucy could poke
her head right through it.

"No answer," said Luke's mum,

replacing the receiver. "Maybe they're out looking for her – OH!"

At that very moment Lucy wriggled out of the hole in the box, and dashed for the open door.

"Come back!" Luke shouted.

Not likely! Lucy thought as she rushed off down the path.

Lucy ran as fast as she could,

until she was sure that Luke and his mum weren't following her. From then on she was careful to scurry out of sight when any humans came along – she really was fed up with kind people trying to help her!

It was a long way to the animal shelter, longer than Lucy had thought it would be. But at last, she turned the corner and saw a big sign with red and blue letters. Lucy couldn't read, but she could recognise the pictures of the cat and dog on the sign. They were the same as the ones on the shirts that the people at the animal shelter wore.

"I made it," Lucy miaowed happily. "Rosie! Rosie! I'm back!"

Chapter Five

Lucy dashed up to the gates of the shelter. They were always kept locked so that none of the animals could escape and get lost. But that didn't stop Lucy. There was a very small gap at the bottom of the gate, but it was just about big enough for Lucy to

squeeze under. Then she
scampered happily off towards
the cat pens.

"Rosie! Rosie!" she yowled.

Rosie was curled up in a corner
of her pen, feeling miserable. She
had missed Lucy very much since
her sister had found a new home.
She hated having no one to play
with, and no one to snuggle up to
when she went to sleep.

Then, all of a sudden, as if by
magic, she heard Lucy's voice
and smelled Lucy's smell. For a
moment Rosie thought she was
dreaming. She rushed to the front
of the pen, and saw Lucy racing
towards her, tail waving madly.

"Lucy!" Rosie gasped. "It's you!
It's really you!"

"Of course it's me," Lucy mewed. She tried to nuzzle Rosie through the wire mesh, licking her sister's nose with her pink tongue. "I've come back!"

By now all the other cats in all the pens, including Ginger, Tammy and Winston, had also come to see what was going on.

"What are *you* doing here?"
Winston asked Lucy. "You've got
a new home!"

"But I wanted to come back!"
Lucy explained.

The other cats were amazed,
and began to mutter and miaow
to each other. They'd never heard
of any cat *wanting* to come back
to the shelter when they had a
new home to go to!

"What *is* all this noise?" John
came out of the office, and looked
along the row of cat pens.
"Goodness me!" he gasped as he
spotted a kitten on the wrong
side of the wire mesh. "Is that
Lucy?"

"Yes, it is!" Lucy mewed.

"What on earth are you doing

here?" John asked. He frowned as he scooped Lucy up, and looked at her closely. "I'd better go and ring the Carters at once."

He pulled out his keys, and put Lucy back into her old pen with Rosie and the other cats. Then he hurried back to the office.

"I can't believe you came back," Rosie said joyfully, as she and Lucy rubbed their heads together affectionately. "Didn't you like your new home?"

"Yes, I did . . ." Lucy mewed. But although she was thrilled to see Rosie again, Lucy was now starting to feel rather worried. She had grown to love Charlie over the last week, and she liked her new home. She didn't want to live at the animal shelter again. What she *really* wanted was for Rosie to come and live at the Carters' house too. But how could she make Charlie understand that?

Lucy began to feel even more worried when, a little while later, she saw Charlie and her parents coming towards the pen with John. She and Rosie were curled up in their bed together, giving each other a wash, but as soon as Lucy spotted them, she scrambled to her feet and began to mew worriedly. She could see that Charlie was carrying a new cat basket. They'd come to collect her.

"Oh, Lucy," said Charlie sadly,

as John unlocked the pen. "Why did you come back here? Didn't you like living with us?"

Lucy felt very bad indeed when she saw how unhappy Charlie looked. "I didn't mean to upset you," she miaowed quietly, "I just wanted to see my sister, that's all."

The Carters and John came into the pen. "Come on, Lucy, time to go – again!" said John, bending down to pick her up.

"No, wait," said Charlie, stroking Lucy's head. "I don't want to take Lucy away, if she doesn't *want* to live with us."

"But I *do* want to live with you!" Lucy said loudly, "I just want Rosie to come too!" And she dashed over to Rosie, then looked up at Charlie and her parents with pleading eyes.

"Is that other kitten Lucy's friend?" Charlie asked, pointing at Rosie. "Lucy seems to like her a lot."

"Oh, she's Lucy's sister," John explained. "They've been together since they were born."

Charlie's face lit up.

"Oh!" she exclaimed. "Mum, Dad, now I know why Lucy's been so lonely – she's been missing her sister!"

Chapter Six

When Lucy heard Charlie say that, she gave a great miaow and rushed over to her. It had taken a while, but people *did* sometimes understand after all!

"Oh, Charlie," laughed Mrs Carter, "Lucy and Rosie are just kittens!"

"No, Lucy's lonely because she
misses her sister!" Charlie
insisted. "Just – just like I miss
Sam," she added in a wobbly
voice.

Lucy pawed urgently at
Charlie's leg, and Rosie did the
same. Charlie bent down and
picked both of the kittens up.

"They certainly are pretty close," John added. "They've never been separated before."

"See?" Charlie turned to look pleadingly at her parents. "Mum, Dad, do you think . . . ?"

Lucy and Rosie both stared at Mr and Mrs Carter with wide anxious eyes.

Charlie's parents glanced at each other. "We weren't exactly expecting *two* kittens," said Mrs Carter.

"Rosie won't be any trouble," Charlie said quickly. "I'll look after both of them."

"And it's always best to have two kittens if you possibly can," John added. "Then they can amuse each other."

"That's true," said Mrs Carter thoughtfully.

"I don't suppose two kittens will be much more trouble than one," Mr Carter said with a smile.

"YES!" Charlie yelled, and hugged Lucy and Rosie close to her.

"YES!" miaowed Lucy and Rosie together.

So, for the second time, Lucy was taken away from the animal shelter to her new home, but this time Rosie went with her. This time Lucy wasn't lonely and miserable, instead she was tucked up snugly in the same basket as Rosie.

When the car pulled up outside the Carters' house, there was another surprise. The door opened, and Sam came out.

"Sam!" Charlie yelled delightedly as she climbed out of the car, holding the cat basket carefully. "What are you doing here? Look at our kittens!"

"Oh, they're gorgeous!" Sam cried. She took the basket from Charlie so she could get a good look at Lucy and Rosie.

"You didn't say you were coming home this weekend, Sam," said Mrs Carter.

Sam turned pink. "Well, I kind of missed everyone . . ." she confessed.

"Let's go in, and play with the kittens," Charlie said, trying to take the basket from Sam.

"No, I'll carry them inside," Sam insisted, hanging on to the basket.

"No, I will!" Charlie argued.

Their parents laughed. "Why can't you two get on, like Lucy and Rosie do?" Mrs Carter asked.

"OK, we'll both carry it!" Sam grinned, and she and Charlie took the basket into the house together.

"This is our new home," Lucy announced, nipping Rosie's ear affectionately.

"Don't do that!" Rosie laughed, and next second the two kittens were rolling around in their basket, pretending to fight.

Having a sister is the best thing in the whole world! Lucy thought happily. And she was glad that Charlie thought so too!